Pushkin Children's Books
71-75 Shelton Street
London WC2H 9JQ

Vitello Wants a Dad
Original Text: © Kim Fupz Aakeson and Gyldendal, 2008
Illustrations: © Niels Bo Bojesen and Gyldendal, 2008
English translation © Ruth Garde 2013
Published in the United Kingdom by agreement
with the Gyldendal Group Agency, Denmark

This edition published by Pushkin Children's Books in 2013

1 2 3 4 5 6 2015 2014 2013

ISBN 978-1-78269-004-7

Printed in China by WKT Co
www.pushkinpress.com

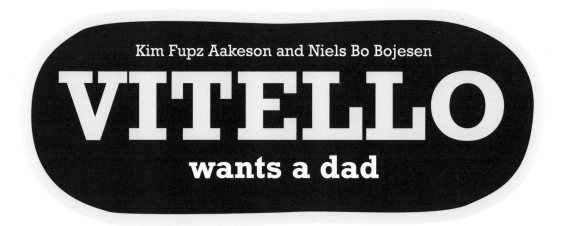

Kim Fupz Aakeson and Niels Bo Bojesen

VITELLO

wants a dad

Translated by Ruth Garde

Pushkin Children's Books

The boy called Vitello lived with his Mum in a terraced house right next to the ring road. The traffic was quite noisy, but it was so central. Mum and Vitello had a nearly new Audi, and there was only one scratch on the paintwork. Mrs Wiedemann lived next door with a very fat cat. So was she. Very fat, that is. The neighbours on the other side were from another country, and nobody knew their names. Quite a lot of other people lived in the other houses.

But nobody saw that much of Vitello's dad. In fact, nobody saw him at all. He was a good-for-nothing, you see. Mum often said: "Your dad is a good-for-nothing, and that's that."

"When I grow up, I'm going to be a good-for-nothing too," said Vitello. "And have a knife."

"You can forget that right now," said Mum.

The other kids in the other houses had dads.
Some of them did, anyway. Max and Harry, the
twins at number 7, had a tall skinny dad who
washed his car a lot. That car was shiny all
right. And he could whistle quite loudly while
he was doing it.

"Where's your dad?" asked Max one day. Or maybe it was Harry who asked—those two were so alike. But if it wasn't one it was the other.

"He's around," said Vitello. Because suddenly he thought it was quite annoying that he didn't have a dad who would wash their Audi and whistle loudly.

"I suppose your mum and dad are divorced," said Harry or Max.

"Not really," said Vitello. "Not very much."

"Where is he, then?" asked Max or Harry.

"Yeah… " nodded Vitello.

"Yeah what?"

"Yeah, you'll see soon enough." That's what Vitello ended up telling Max and Harry. Maybe it wasn't such a smart thing to say. Because how on earth were they going see?

When Mum and Vitello were eating spaghetti with butter and grated cheese that evening, Vitello had a big smile all over his face.

"What's with the silly grin?" asked Mum.

"I was thinking about something funny," said Vitello. Mum didn't ask what.

Vitello said, "I was thinking that it would be funny if we invited my dad over for spaghetti one night."

"Your dad?" Mum looked at Vitello, raising her eyebrows. "Forget about him."

"I don't even know him," said Vitello.

"So much the easier to forget about him," said Mum.

"Hmph," said Vitello.

Mum told him to shush, and they ate their spaghetti with butter and grated cheese without saying another word.

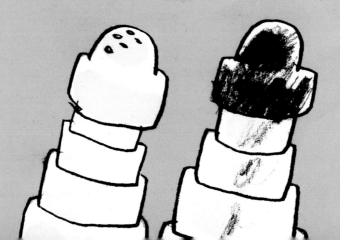

Vitello needed to get himself a dad. Just to borrow, just someone he could show to Harry and Max. He could probably find a decent dad in the shopping centre. There were usually quite a few men down there.

He was right. Even before he got into the shopping centre Vitello found a quite acceptable one in the car park. He was wearing a suit and had a supercool car that was really shiny and clean. He was standing in front of his cool car talking on his mobile. Vitello stood next to him to see how it would feel to have that kind of dad. It felt pretty good.

The man was talking loudly on his mobile. He said, "What the hell is that supposed to mean, Tony? Do I have 'Idiot' on my forehead?"

"Heehee," laughed Vitello. Nice to have a dad who swore a bit.

"Tony, I'll ask you again. Do I have 'Idiot' on my forehead?" Then he hung up.

"Don't worry. It doesn't say anything on your forehead," said Vitello.

The man looked down crossly at Vitello and said: "What are you hanging around here for?"

"I wondered if you could be my dad for a bit?" Vitello asked. "Just while I show you to Max and Harry."

"Who the hell are Max and Harry?"

"Their dad's skinny and washes his car a lot."
Vitello smiled.

"The kid's got a screw loose!" said the man,
and got into his car and sped off.

"Hmmm," said Vitello, thinking it would be
nice to have a dad who was a bit more polite.

The next man was an electrician who was wearing a cap. He was holding a ladder for another electrician who was at the top fixing some cables on a neon sign. Vitello stood near the electrician and smiled. Then he stood a bit closer, then a bit closer still. When he was very close the electrician said "Watch it, kid. Something might fall on you."

"Okay, Dad," said Vitello.

"What did you say?" the electrician asked, staring at Vitello.

"Okay."

"And after that?"

"Dad," mumbled Vitello.

"What's your name?"

"Vitello," said Vitello.

"Listen," said the electrician.
"I've got a boy called Ronnie, and
a boy called Kyle. I'm pretty sure I
haven't got one called Vitello."

"That's a shame," said Vitello. "You see I need a dad to show my friends. The one I've got is a good-for-nothing, and he never comes to visit me and Mum, and Mum won't invite him over for spaghetti and says I have to forget about him, but I can't because I've never seen him."

The electrician looked as if he had got
something in his eye. Or in both eyes. He kept
on wiping them and cleared his throat twice.

"Are you holding that ladder or what?"
shouted his mate from the top of the ladder.

"Clear off, kid," said the electrician, nodding
towards a bag lying against the wall. "You can
take that bag of empty bottles with you."

"Why?" asked Vitello.

"Because you can get money for recycling
the bottles and then buy something, you nitwit."

"Oh," said Vitello. It was better than nothing.

Vitello got enough money for the empty bottles to buy himself a hot dog, so he went to the hot dog stand behind the shopping centre and looked at the pictures on the menu.

"What would you like, son?" asked the hot dog man.

"I'm not actually hungry," said Vitello, and sighed.

"One hot dog coming right up," said the hot dog man. "Mustard and ketchup, son?"

"Naah," said Vitello. "I don't want anything at all."

The hot dog man smiled and squeezed loads of mustard and ketchup onto the hot dog and said, "There you go, son. One pound eighty, please."

"You're a bit deaf, aren't you?" said Vitello.

"Fried onions coming right up." The hot dog man scooped a pile of fried onions next to the ketchup and the mustard and the hot dog. "Here you go, son."

Vitello thought for a moment. Then he smiled and put the money on the counter.

Afterwards he went to fetch
Max and Harry. They dawdled
along behind him all the way
to the hot dog stand. Vitello
stopped and pointed. "That's
my dad over there," he said.

"The hot dog man?" asked
Max. Or Harry.

Vitello waved to the hot dog
man and shouted, "Hi, Dad!"

The hot dog man waved
back and shouted, "Hi, son!"

"Wow," said Harry. Or Max. "Does he give out free hot dogs?"

"Not to kids he doesn't know," said Vitello. "Just to me, his beloved son."

Harry and Max thought that seemed fair enough.

"See you, Dad!" shouted Vitello, and waved again.

"Take care, son," shouted the hot dog man.

"Pretty cool to have a dad with a hot dog stand," said Max, or Harry, on the way home.

"Yup, really pretty cool," said the boy called Vitello. And then they didn't say another word about it.